The Old Woman Inside

AuthorHouse™
1663 Liberty Drive
Bloomington, IN 47403
www.authorhouse.com
Phone: 1 (800) 839-8640

Published by AuthorHouse 12/20/2018

ISBN: 978-1-5462-7254-0 (sc)
ISBN: 978-1-5462-7253-3 (e)

Library of Congress Control Number: 2018914882

Print information available on the last page.

authorHOUSE®

The Old Woman Inside

....

DEBBIE VIALE

There was an old woman where we used to play. She lived in this old house, alone, every day.

Our parents told us it wasn't safe and to stay away from that old place.

Now we sneak in a group of kids hoping to see something lurk in the night then running like the dickens and screeching from the fright. Hoping to find the old woman inside.

Her death wasn't possible. Our friends must have lied. We saw her shadow from the window outside. We shouted out riddles then ran out of sight.

Now everyone knows
about the old woman.

Kids come in groups and watch in the night.

I, too, want to see her, there's chills down my spine.

I pass by each morning on my way to school.

Everyone shouts, "Isn't that cruel?"

Finally, I got up enough nerve as I passed. I knocked at the door while holding her cat. I said that I found a cat just outside.

Then she opened the window and whispered its name. "Boots likes to wander like the children," she explained. So I introduced myself and gave her the cat.

Then I ran home to tell mother about the old woman. She will give me a lecture and say, "Stay away!"

But the old woman inside wasn't put there to hide. She's lonely, and shy, and no one cares why. I think I'll go get her and make her my friend. Bring her home for a meal and give her a hand.

About the Author

I grew up in a small town by the San Francisco Bay "Martinez" Ca. I started writing at age 14 and published many poems through the years. I'm living on a Horse Ranch now and use alot of my short stories to entertain my 5 grandchildren. So I decided to publish several stories they enjoy.